How Do You Go to Sleep?

by Kate McMullan   illustrated by Sydney Hanson

Alfred A. Knopf   New York

Squirrel curls up inside her den
within a hollow tree.

Octopus changes color
as he slumbers undersea.

Parrot stands on one foot,
his head tucked in his feathers.

Meerkat sleeps in a heap
of family all together.

How do YOU go to sleep?

Is a tree your
cozy bed?

Do you turn
purple, orange,
and red?

Rest your head
upon your back?

Sleep with others
in a stack?
NO!

Zebra locks his knees and stays standing up all night.

Tiger naps in leafy shade
to hide her stripes from sight.

Frog hibernates all winter
under snow so deep.

Dolphin shuts just one eye
and goes swimming in her sleep.

How do YOU go to sleep?

Do you stand and
lock your knees?

Is your bed beneath
the leaves?

Is your blanket
made of snow?

Do you sleep-swim
to and fro?
NO!

Mouse digs a tunnel,
then she snoozes underground.

Pigeon perches with his friends
where shelter can be found.

Seal pokes out her snout
and doze-floats in the bay.

Skunk runs around all night,
then sleeps the day away.

How do YOU go to sleep?

Do you burrow
underground?

Roost with all your
pals around?

Do you float until
the dawn?

Does the sunrise
make you yawn?
NO!

Well, when you go to bed,
if you don't sleep
a tree sleep or sea sleep,
a tuck sleep or heap sleep,
a stand sleep or leaf sleep,
a snow sleep or swim sleep,
a nest sleep or perch sleep,
a float sleep or sun sleep,
how DO you go to sleep?

Do you first turn
off the light?

Do you wish the moon
good night?

Do you close your
tired eyes?
Listen to some
lullabies?

Do you think about your day,
And all the fun you had at play?
Do you hug and kiss kiss kiss?
Do you go to sleep like THIS?

Yesssssssssssszzzzzzzzzzzzzzzzzz.

For Arthur & Lily —K.M.

For Ava Lou —S.H.

THIS IS A BORZOI BOOK PUBLISHED BY ALFRED A. KNOPF

Text copyright © 2019 by Kate McMullan
Jacket art and illustrations copyright © 2019 by Sydney Hanson
All rights reserved. Published in the United States by Alfred A. Knopf, an imprint of
Random House Children's Books, a division of Penguin Random House LLC, New York.
Knopf, Borzoi Books, and the colophon are registered trademarks of Penguin Random House LLC.

Visit us on the Web! rhcbooks.com
Educators and librarians, for a variety of teaching tools, visit us at RHTeachersLibrarians.com

Library of Congress Cataloging-in-Publication Data is available upon request.
ISBN 978-0-525-57944-1 (trade)
ISBN 978-0-525-57945-8 (lib. bdg.)
ISBN 978-0-525-57946-5 (ebook)

The illustrations in this book were created using mixed media.
MANUFACTURED IN CHINA
October 2019   10 9 8 7 6 5 4 3 2 1   First Edition